I'M HIS PROPERTY

Dark Hucow BDSM

Leandra Camilli

CONTENTS

CHAPTER 1

He took my hand. His grip was strong. I felt his fingers around mine, and I couldn't do anything. I couldn't do anything because I was naked and also because I could feel his eyes boring into me, making me feel more uncomfortable than I already was.

"It's so nice that you have come here," he said. His name was Mr. Lawrence. For the time being, that was his name to me. The only name that I could use and that I could think of whenever I thought about him.

He was imperious. He was so much taller than me that I could wrap my arms around him and they would go under his armpits. He could rest his chin on top of my head, and he would be able to do that without going on his tiptoes.

He could make me feel so small with his body, which was something I never thought I would be feeling now that I was a hucow. I had gone through the transformation, and now here I was, about to be sold to him.

"Yeah, we had to come. We want to sell her and you said on the website that you were interested," my associate said. His name was Jake and he was here to sell me to Mr. Lawrence. He was a good guy and I was certain that he was going to do his best for the sales pitch, no doubt about it.

Mr. Lawrence eyed me up and down, his eyes scanning my body.

They rested on my boobs. That was what he wanted to see, wasn't it? The thing that he was waiting for the most. I was certain that was the case, and it was a reason for me to be proud of myself.

I had worked so hard to make my boobs as big as they could be, and it worked. My boobs were so big now that his hands would feel small when he started to play with them, I thought, hiding the smile that wanted to creep up on my face.

"Yeah, I said that. She really is something else, isn't she?" He asked, his eyes still lingering on my boobs. It felt like they would never stop staring at them, and that just might turn out to be the case, I thought, squirming my legs together.

My associate put his hand on my shoulder, stroking it. "We did everything possible to make it so she really fits your needs," he said, smiling devilishly. He had all the reasons to be smiling like that, even though we knew that nothing would happen between us.

He had always said he felt something for me, but I was certain that it was nothing more than just a hucow-associate crush, and it would never lead to anything.

"I can see that you did. Her breasts are so big, so perky, and they look heavy, too," Mr. Lawrence said, and I could tell that the only thing he wanted to do right now was to be with his hands all over me.

In the meantime, I couldn't help but look down, seeing his cock under his pants. He wasn't doing anything to hide his erection, and that wasn't surprising. He knew he was on top of everything and that I was going to do everything he wanted, even though there was going to be a safe word that we were going to decide on later.

"We really outdid ourselves when transforming her," Jake said, his hand moving down and making me wonder if he was going to do what I was thinking he was. Cupping my ass. His hand was close, but it wasn't quite there yet, I thought.

"Yeah, you really did," Mr. Lawrence said, stepping to the side and holding out his hand. He was inviting us inside his house. "Please, come in. Let's sit down and have something to drink."

His house? I thought, realizing how stupid I was. It was more like a mansion. It was big. It was impressive. It was fit for a billionaire, and I couldn't help but feel I was out of place here. I pretty much was, I thought.

I would never live in a place quite like this, and that was a given.

Either way, this was going to be my new house. Just on the far side, I noticed a portrait hanging above the fireplace. It showed Mr. Lawrence and Mrs. Lawrence, his wife.

I didn't know her, and I actually also didn't know much about Mr. Lawrence, either. He was walking in front of us, leading us inside the house. We were in the main hall, and from here we could reach the second floor of the house. I felt so small in this place, and I knew it would take me a lot of time to get used to it.

"Whoa," I said, looking around and almost tripping and losing my balance. Thankfully, that didn't happen. Had that happened, I would be so flustered and looking so confused I would never know where to bury my head.

"This is all mine," Mr. Lawrence said as if it needed to be said. Of course it was all his.

We reached what appeared to be the living room in the house. He sat down, ordered one of the waiters to bring us something to drink, and I couldn't focus on anything that he said. Either way, I knew that it was going to be something nice. Something to break the ice between us.

He sat down with his legs spread apart, his erection still showing under his pants.

As if to show me that this was his dominion, his territory, he held nothing back before putting his fingers under his pants, starting to stroke his hardness. Wow.

I didn't think he was just going to start doing that, and it was hot. It was a turn-on, and I suddenly found myself even more flustered than before. I knew that he could see the red tint on my cheeks.

And he was smiling devilishly without showing his teeth.

CHAPTER 2

Even Jake was a little taken aback by what his eyes were seeing. He didn't think that his customer was simply going to start pumping his cock in front of us. And he was doing it slowly, making sure that his eyes lingered on me. I knew why he was doing that. He wanted me to feel more wetness in my pussy, and it was working.

I couldn't help but squirm my legs together.

Was this really happening? I asked myself. I blinked twice, not really believing it. The first moment when I had seen Mr. Lawrence, I thought that he was someone that behaved well, someone that put his self-image above everything else when it came to meeting new people, but that didn't appear to be the case.

Either that, or he thought that Jake wasn't going to leave his house anytime soon.

I turned my head to the side, finding him. His eyes were wide. He couldn't believe what he was seeing, I thought.

But there was something else going on here. Looking down, I found his erection. He was… Turned on by what he was seeing? I asked myself, but it wasn't really a question. It was more like a statement.

It was true. He was turned on by what his eyes were seeing. After turning my head back to the other side, I noticed that Mr. Lawrence was smiling more devilishly than before.

He was such a prick, but it was exactly for that reason that I felt turned on. I just had a thing for bad boys, and I knew that would never change.

"Mr. Lawrence… As I was saying, I'm really happy that you've decided to buy Jenna," he said, mentioning my name.

"I'm really happy about that, too," Mr. Lawrence said, his hand still moving up and down slowly along his cock. It was so massive that it took him a couple seconds to finish each movement. I couldn't help but wonder if it would even be possible for me to put it all inside my mouth. "But that doesn't matter anymore. The money will fall into your bank account when the time is right, and when you do something for me."

"Do… Something for you?" Jake asked, his hand shaking. It was the first time that I was seeing him so nervous. It was like he didn't know what to do with his hands. And his face was pale, too.

Mr. Lawrence lifted his hand – the one that he wasn't using to pump his cock. "Stand up."

"What?" Jake asked, not believing what he had just heard.

Mr. Lawrence narrowed his eyes slightly, furrowing his brow. "I said, stand up. I want you to suck me off."

There was a moment of silence. Jake was still processing what his ears heard.

"Mr. Lawrence, but I don't understand. I thought that the transaction was already finished. I thought that you had already made up your mind about it."

"I have, but I need to warm up. Come closer. I know that you want to do this."

"But I'm not gay!" Jake stated, fisting his hand. Wow. Where did that come from? I asked myself, suddenly finding it unlikely that he had grown a backbone in so little time.

Mr. Lawrence took a deep breath. He didn't look pleased by what was happening at all.

"Come here, or I'm going to spank you," Mr. Lawrence threatened, and I knew that he meant it. He meant each and every single one of his words, and that was putting it mildly.

"I suppose that to make sure that the transaction will happen the way it should, I should really do this," Jake murmured, unclenching his hand. I was surprised by this, more than anything, and I suddenly found myself with my hand already stroking my clit.

"Yeah, you should really do this, or I'm really going to spank you. You don't want to know how hard I can spank someone," Mr. Lawrence threatened, and then I saw Jake dragging himself over to Mr. Lawrence.

The latter stood up, lowering his pants and his pair of boxer briefs.

When he did that, I gasped. I covered my mouth with my hand, but it was already too late. He noticed it. He noticed that I was impressed by the size of his cock, and I was certain he was going to use that knowledge to his advantage when he had his eyes and attention set on me.

For the time being, I didn't really have to worry much about that.

This was Jake's turn to please him.

"What do you want me to do, master?" Jake asked, and I noticed that his voice was a lot throatier and heavier than normal. It was like he had lost the person that he used to be and that he would never recover it. It was all thanks to the way that Mr. Lawrence bored his eyes into him.

"Get on your knees and suck me off," Mr. Lawrence ordered, sitting back down on the couch.

His legs were so thick and hairy, and that only made me salivate more than I already was.

"Yes, master," Jake said, slowly getting on his knees in front of Mr. Lawrence, who was more than happy to put his hand on his head, guiding it down slowly and into his cock.

Fuck. This was really happening and I had to blink a couple of times to make sure that I wasn't imagining things. And yeah, this was really happening, and I was already witnessing gay sex on my first day here in Mr. Lawrence's house.

His eyes were focused only on Jake, and this was really the first time that I was seeing a man completely submitting himself to another, and the only thing that it was making me do was to start to rub my clit more feverishly.

If this continued to happen the way it was, I was going to come without doing anything else.

CHAPTER 3

My body was getting hotter. Sweat was beginning to cover my skin, and I could already start to hear the wet sounds filling the air. Jake had his lips around Mr. Lawrence's cock, moving his head up and down slowly, running his tongue around it, making sure that he was doing this slowly and nicely.

I just had no idea that he could suck off someone so efficiently, showing so much skill.

And in the meantime, I was rubbing my clit, my finger moving up and down, left and right, slowly and sometimes I did the same but faster, too.

My body was beginning to get so much hotter, and my breathing was starting to feel heavy.

Then, Mr. Lawrence looked up, finding me. He had his attention focused on me, and I didn't know what to do. All I knew was that I had to keep moving my finger up and down, making sure that I was bringing myself closer to my orgasm.

He was still smiling devilishly, showing me how overconfident he was.

"You are really enjoying this, aren't you, Jenna?" He asked, his voice low and threatening.

I nodded. It was the only thing I could do right now, and he was pleased by that.

"Are you going to come all over his face?" I asked quickly.

He widened his smile slightly. "I might do that, or I might do something else. It really all depends on what I want to do when I feel it finally coming out," he replied.

And in the meantime, Jake was still bobbing up and down on him, spreading as much of his saliva as he could around his master's massive prick, making sure that his pace was slow so that he pleased Mr. Lawrence as much as possible.

Mr. Lawrence returned his attention to his sub, moving his fingers in his hair, and then after gripping some of it, he started to dictate the pace even more strongly than before.

"This is really nice, what you are doing, but I want something else," he purred, making me wonder what that was.

He pulled his hand up, pulling back Jake's head. The latter looked up with pleading eyes, and I noticed that they were gleaming with tears.

"What else do you want me to do for you, master?" Jake asked, his voice sounding so submissive, as if he was nothing in comparison to the much bigger man before him.

"I want you to take everything inside your mouth."

"What?" Jake asked, not believing what he had just heard.

"Do you want me to repeat myself? I'm already pissed that you didn't hear me the first time," he said, his voice threatening.

Jake looked down. "No, I'm sorry, master."

"So, do it already."

"Yes, master," Jake responded, lowering his head and wrapping his lips around Mr. Lawrence's prick, who himself tilted his head back, showing that he was enjoying what was being done to him.

"Yeah, that's it. Fuck, that's the spot," he said and I could see that it spurred Jake on, who was now sucking him off more feverishly, and as for me, I couldn't stop scrubbing my clit with my finger, and I also felt my body slumping into the couch. I could feel my climax coming and when it finally broke out, I knew that it would wash over my entire body, making me feel like I hadn't in a very long time.

Time was passing slowly and also fast at the same time, and I had no idea anymore what was happening, just that it was good.

Just when I was about to reach my climax, Mr. Lawrence pulled Jake's head back up, shooting up from the couch, and then he aimed his cock at his sub's face.

A moment later, it started to happen. He started to shoot his load all over Jake's face, who himself had closed his eyes and was taking everything without complaining. He was actually feeling the opposite of that. He was proud of himself. I could see that in the smile on his face.

His sacrifice was going to be worth it.

He had just managed to sell me to Mr. Lawrence, and that was everything he wanted.

I could see Mr. Lawrence's load hitting his cheeks, his nose, his forehead, and his jaw. He was painting his sub's face in white, and it was absolutely jaw-dropping.

Jake had submitted himself completely to the much bigger, more imposing man, and I had never seen anything quite like this. So much so that it finally brought me over the edge, and I finally came.

My body started to shudder, shake, and tremble violently.

I pulled my hand back up and reopened my eyes slowly, soon finding out that Jake was already swiping his tongue over the sides of his mouth as quickly as he could, swallowing as much of Mr. Lawrence's sperm as possible.

Mr. Lawrence shook his cock one last time, making sure that he had emptied everything he had in his balls.

When Jake reopened his eyes, he asked, "Was that everything you wanted, master?"

"Not quite. You still have to clean up the mess you made," the master explained, smirking.

For some reason, I knew he was going to say that.

Jake gulped, but I knew he was still going to do it, thus it wasn't surprising when he lowered his head one more time, using his tongue to clean Mr. Lawrence's dick as best as he could and as efficiently as possible, and also without ruining everything he had done right so far.

When he was done, I could see it on his face. He loved what happened, even though he would never admit that through his words.

"Now that it's over, you can leave," Mr. Lawrence stated, which was relieving for Jake, who didn't stop himself before cleaning his face with his hands, licking his fingers clean. He loved the taste of his master's cum, didn't he?

He didn't even look at me before bolting out of the house, leaving me alone with Mr. Lawrence.

I knew that now it was my turn, and part of me was scared, but another part of me was also excited.

Much more so than I had ever been in my life, in fact.

CHAPTER 4

I was still in the living room and I noticed that Mr. Lawrence was looking at me. He still had that same devilish smile on his face, and I knew he had plans for me.

I felt shivers running down my spine.

"Stand up. You are my property and you do exactly everything I want," he stated, and I knew it was the truth.

I stood up slowly and he stepped toward me. He stood so imperiously in front of me. He placed his hands on my shoulders, sliding them down slowly over my arms. He was feeling the softness and smoothness of my skin.

"Yes, master. I'm your property and I always do exactly everything you want," I stated and he nodded in approval.

"Good girl. I'm going to take you somewhere where we can finally start things the way they should," he explained, taking his hands off my shoulders, which was disappointing.

I glanced down at his cock, wishing to put it between my lips. It was such a pity that it wasn't going to happen – at least, not at this moment.

I followed him. I had no idea where he was thinking he was going, but it was somewhere deep in his house. Deep underground, I noticed.

A couple of minutes later, we finally stood in front of a door. The door led to a room much bigger than I thought it was. And everything was dark and I could also see some torches hanging from the walls.

"This is my sex dungeon," he said, taking off his clothes and standing naked in front of me. It was a pity that I couldn't see his body in full detail. I wished we were doing this outside so that it was happening that way, but I wasn't going to complain.

Mr. Lawrence was hard again and even though he had just come not too long ago, I knew he could do it again and I also knew it would be as potent as it was before.

"You're so pretty. Jake said that you are a virgin. Is that right?" He asked, moving with me over to a certain machine that stood by one of the walls in the dungeon.

Even though it was just my first time seeing this model, I knew what it was for. To milk me. Mr. Lawrence was going to empty my jugs, and I couldn't wait anymore for that. My pussy was already throbbing in anticipation.

"Yes, master. I am a virgin."

"Good. That means he didn't try to rip me off, which would have been very unfortunate for him," he explained, helping me with putting me in the machine.

The way that I was put in the machine, I was lying down in it, my body like it was floating in the air. Then, he also attached two cups to my boobs and turned on the machine, which made it start to whir almost like it was happy. Happy that I was in it…

"How do you feel, being milked like this?" He probed, placing his hand on my back and stroking it, moving it slowly and nicely. I wasn't going to deny that just that was enough to get me going again, and that wicked smile on his face… It showed me that he wanted me to be feeling exactly this way.

In the meantime, I couldn't stop stealing glances at his mesmerizing cock, which was so big and was pointing right at me, right to my face. It was so sad that I couldn't wrap my lips around it, which was exactly what I wanted to be doing at the moment.

As the machine continued to work and milk me, I replied, "Better than ever, master." Master Lawrence nodded in approval.

"Good. There's definitely something I think we should already deal with," he said, positioning himself behind me. I wondered what he meant the moment when he started to prod my pussy with his cockhead.

I felt a tingle of excitement traveling in my body, and then it was replaced by pain when he finally started to penetrate me. One inch at a time, master Lawrence only stopped when he met my hymen. When he did that, I thought that Mr. Lawrence was going to ask me again how I felt, but he didn't.

"Oh fuck, this is the spot, isn't it?" He asked, a moment later pushing right through it, finally taking my virginity. I already knew he was going to do it, but it still came as a surprise to me, and it was absolutely devastating, and I came then and there.

My body started to shake and it was only minutes later when it finally stopped. It had already been a couple of minutes since the machine started to milk me, and I could feel my breasts getting empty.

"Yes, master, that was exactly the spot," I cooed and he started to cackle and laugh.

"Good Lord, Jenna, you're already so submissive and addicted to my cock," he said without hiding how overconfident he was and that, instead of annoying me, made me actually want more of this.

"Yes, master, I'm always submissive and exactly everything you want," I said and he held nothing back as he started to pound in and out of me, his pace frenetic from the get-go.

I started to match his rhythm thrust for thrust, and I came one more time, smearing his dick with my cunt juice, which I could tell he loved.

And then, master Lawrence finally erupted inside of me. He was knocking me up, and the thought alone was enough to make me start to squeal and moo.

I knew that my master was always going to impregnate me, but now that it was happening, it was another thing entirely.

It was much better than my expectations for it were.

CHAPTER 5

Minutes later, it had all ended, and I was here with my master, still in the sex dungeon. He was still right behind me and even after he came, he refused to pull out of me. To be honest, that was equally surprising and terrifying.

It wasn't just that I was addicted to his cock, but that he was also becoming addicted to my pussy.

"It's so warm in here I don't want to leave," he stated, jamming his prick even further inside of me, going all the way in. And after he did that, I noticed his prick shooting out another rope of come.

Mr. Lawrence didn't just make sure that I was pregnant, but also that I was going to be feeling a lot of pain in the coming days. Even walking was going to be almost impossible, but I didn't feel worried about that.

"Please, don't leave, master," I begged and even though I couldn't see his face, not even in a reflection anywhere, I was still certain that he was smiling devilishly at me.

A moment later, he explained, "You know, my wife and I… We never did anything like this together. She just doesn't want to do it, which forced my hand to be doing this."

"Master, I'm just happy that I'm making you happy," I said and then he finally pulled out. I had to admit I wasn't looking forward to this moment. When he wasn't inside of me anymore, I was sad.

"I'm happy that you can make that happen," he said, walking until he stood in front of me.

When I was going to open my mouth to say something, he said, "I should have gagged you."

"Why didn't you do it?" I asked and he chuckled, turning his back to me, and now I could finally see, for the first time, how perfect and mesmerizing his ass was. It was such a pity that he would never let me touch it. I couldn't help but wonder if his wife had gotten a taste of it.

Just when I was going to wonder about that some more, he turned around and this time he held something in his hand. It was a ball gag, and after seeing it, my body already started to feel so excited.

"It turns out that sometimes I forget some things," he explained as he put the ball gag in my mouth, making sure that the back part of it was nicely secured on my head.

This time, I couldn't speak anything, and I knew that the ball gag meant that he was going to do something even more painful than before. I couldn't help but wonder what that was.

He took a step back, placing his fingers around his prick, and then he started to pump it. I was completely entranced where I was, suddenly realizing that the milking machine had already stopped working. It had emptied my breasts, and now my body felt even more like nothing than before.

I was waiting in anticipation when he finally erupted all over my face, shooting rope after rope of come all over it, making sure that he was painting it in white.

When he was done, I noticed the way that his belly was expanding and contracting slowly. This was the third time that he came today, and it felt like some kind of record. Mr. Lawrence was just so virile and potent that it was unbelievable.

"You want even more of this, don't you?" He asked, stepping around the milking machine, positioning himself behind me again. Even though I still felt a lot of pain coming from my ravaged snatch, there was no denying that I could still go for another round.

Another round filled with him penetrating me, going deep inside me, and ascertaining himself that he really got me pregnant today.

I nodded. For the time being, it was the only thing I could do.

A moment later, he held nothing back, placing his hands on my thighs and then digging his fingers into my skin, hurting me more than I already was. Seconds later, he started to touch and feel my entrance with his oversized prick, and then he pushed past it. It was a lot easier than before, and... wow.

I came another time just as he finished doing that. I felt like I was still a virgin, and I knew that it was going to take me so much time to recover from this moment.

Then, Mr. Lawrence started to piston in and out of me, his pace destructive from the get-go, and I could even feel his balls slapping against my ass, which was a good bonus.

One last time, Mr. Lawrence jammed his prick deep inside my womb, and then he stopped when he started to come inside of me again. My teeth bit into the ball gag, and I hated that it was in my mouth, impeding me from squealing and mooing as much as I wanted to.

And yet, this moment was so singular, so pleasing I would never replace it with another.

I still couldn't believe that he was so virile that he was able to come four times today.

When he was done, just like the first time, he refused to pull out of me soon, which this time wasn't surprising.

It was only minutes later when he finally did that, and I noticed something that terrified me. Mr. Lawrence was still hard. He walked until he stood in front of me again, and I knew he wanted to go for another round with me.

But this time, Mr. Lawrence wasn't just going to impregnate me – he was going to do something even more terrifying than before.

And I couldn't help but wait for that.

EPILOGUE

"**W**ho the hell are you?" She asked me the moment she stepped inside where I was. I was in the living room, seated on the couch and with my hands roaming over my belly.

It had been months since I first came here, and now I was with a pregnant belly on full display. That was Mr. Lawrence's wife, and she was fuming. She was looking at me with wide, terrified eyes.

After all, this was the first time she was seeing me here. I was a stranger to her, as I should be. But today my master showed me that he wanted me to reveal myself to his wife.

I didn't know what his plan was, but I was certain that he finally wanted to divorce her.

"I'm his pet. I'm whatever he wants me to be to him, and that is something you can never give him. So, I'm also much better than you. I'm so much better than you when it comes to pleasing Mr. Lawrence."

"I don't know who you are, but I want you out of my house right at this moment," she barked, fisting her hand. I almost thought she was going to try and punch me, but she didn't.

I knew where she was coming from. Germany. She had come from there after a long trip, and now she wanted to find out why I was here.

To be honest, I wasn't much worried about that. I was just happy that I had Mr. Lawrence's child in my belly. It was like I was helping him build his empire.

It was just like he had told me before. This was the first time that he was going to have a child, which was mind-boggling and infuriating. Mrs. Lawrence should be looking at herself and asking herself what exactly happened since she married him. I couldn't know this for sure, but I was almost certain that it was because she wanted him for the money.

"She's not going anywhere, my... *wife*," a thick, deep voice echoed from behind her, and I knew that it was Mr. Lawrence's. He was behind her, I noticed when she turned around in a heartbeat.

"Care to explain exactly what's going on here? Who the fuck is this bitch?" She barked, and it was kind of funny. It was kind of funny the way she thought she had any power here.

"She's my new pet. She is always submissive, she never fights back, and she wants to be my property. I'm not sorry to be saying this, but you are always so overcomplicated that I had to look for an alternative, and now I'm happy that I finally did."

"What?" She asked and I thought that she was going to continue her tantrum against us, but in a moment, she collapsed on the floor, making me feel flabbergasted.

I didn't think she was just going to pass out, but now that she did...

I couldn't help but wonder...

I couldn't help but wonder what my master had in mind for her.

The End

Thank you for reading this story. Leave your review. Your feedback helps me immensely!

TEASER: HANDCUFFED FOR BAD BEHAVIOR

Hucow Milking Story

Not the place where I wanted to be.

Not with these people looking at me.

I mean, I was in the middle of a crowd, but I was still certain that they were looking at me.

Judging me.

Someone was standing on a raised platform and speaking, but I couldn't pay any attention to his words.

I couldn't stop thinking that something had to be wrong with this. All the hucows were women and all the trainers and professors were men.

Obviously, all the hucows were going to be women, but all the teachers were men? What the hell was going on here?

They were keeping us naked in the main hall, and we couldn't do anything about it.

One peep and it would be enough to put us in their cells.

They were cold, unforgiving. I couldn't stand even thinking about those cells, and I was certain that it would never happen to me.

The teachers would never put us in one of those cells.

It didn't matter that they were all smoking hot.

They were never going to make me think that anything could ever happen between us.

Even though…

Even though the reason why I came here was simple.

I thought that I could strike gold by coming here. Thought that one of the teachers would have eyes for me, but that lasted until I realized that they were all married.

And I wasn't lying. All of them had marriage rings on their fingers, destroying all hope that I once had. So why did I even think that coming here was going to solve anything?

The truth was that it wasn't going to solve anything.

We were all here, in the main hall, and the teacher on the raised platform was speaking about what our lives here were going to be like.

It was like time was passing but wasn't at the same time.

I took a deep breath in, closed my eyes, and thought that for sure nothing else was going to happen here.

We were going to be taken to our bedrooms, they were going to lock us in there, and that was going to be it.

I was so certain of that that I wasn't even aware of what was happening around me or what my ears were hearing.

That was why I was so stunned when I noticed someone right by my side, and it wasn't one of the candidates.

It was actually a man. One of the teachers, I noticed right away. He was nothing short of stunning.

He looked just like all the other teachers, but he was also different.

Blond hair.

Stubble on his face.

Square jawline.

Full lips.

A massive, hulky body.

And eyes that looked into mine as though he could read everything I was thinking.

Even though I wasn't even trying to say anything, I felt like I was mumbling. I was so stunned that my body had frozen up. And

I was certain that he was aware of the effect he was having on me. It was why he wasn't smiling right now.

Such a devilish, evil smile, and he wasn't ashamed of it.

And I was certain that he knew how aroused he was making me feel, too.

After all, why else would he be pulling up the side of his lips like that, showing me a little of his teeth? Even though I couldn't see much, there was no denying that they were shining.

"Who are you?" I asked, hoping that he was going to be forthcoming with his answer, but knowing that he didn't have to.

He didn't say anything for the first few seconds, making me feel so anxious, and I was certain he was using that to his advantage as well.

If there was something I learned about the teachers here in Deimour College, it was that they had no boundaries when it came to taking advantage of their students.

"I'm Jason. I'm one of the teachers here in the college," he replied, not giving me any new information. Of course he wouldn't.

"I already knew that," I said, my eyes moving up and down while I felt some wetness and heat between my legs. It was impossible not to be feeling that way when he was so hot and was so incredibly close to me.

He was so close that he was making it difficult for me to breathe.

I just couldn't stop scrutinizing every part of his body.

His rippling muscles.

His bulging biceps.

His crotch.

The way his shirt showed off his abs.

And pretty much everything else. The more I looked at this man, Jason, the more I felt absolutely stunned.

And that made me feel like doing something I thought I never would.

Bad behavior.

Behaving in a way that would put me into trouble.

I knew that was a mistake, but I was still willing to go through with it until the end.

But what would be my punishment if that happened?

"Do you want something from me?" I asked and for the time being, it was like everything happening around me didn't matter anymore.

"I don't know. You tell me."

I checked him out from bottom to top again, my eyes lingering on his crotch. I didn't know if he was wearing tight boxer briefs, but his bulge was so big, and it kept on making me think about what it would be like to feel it with my fingers.

Should I do that? I didn't know, and I was soon realizing that I had to make a decision. After all, the other teacher, whose name I didn't know, was already moving away from the raised platform after speaking his lines in front of the students.

We were all going somewhere else, but I realized that I didn't have to.

After all, Jason was with me.

His eyes were staring at me.

"I think you know what I want from you, and I think you also know why you came here."

He was so sure of himself that it was maddening, and it still melted my heart.

Could I really not do what he wanted? The more time passed here, the more I realized that it was impossible not to.

Thus, without giving it a second thought, I just moved away with him somewhere else.

But we weren't going with the other teachers and the students. We were going to a separate room in Deimour College, and I couldn't wait for some sexy time with Jason.

I knew he was unbelievably hung.

SIMILAR BOOKS

BUNDLE - HUCOW PRISON

All the books of the Hucow Prison series in one single, convenient collection.

1. Hucow Prison

SERIES - BUMPED HUCOWS

1. Milked by Rockstars

2. Tamed by Rockstars

3. Taken by Rockstars

4. Claimed by Rockstars

SERIES - HIS HERD

1. Peculiar Dairy

2. Milked by her Boyfriend

3. Menage for Milking

4. Farm Milking

5. Fertile for my Farmers

ABOUT THE AUTHOR

Leandra Camilli's obsession? Writing dirty, steamy stories that make her readers drool. She loves her Alpha males, hucows, sissies, and futas. If you're looking for those kinds of books, look no further.

With a cup of coffee on her table and warm socks on, she writes almost every day. Leandra Camilli has featured in several top 100 categories in the store, and she publishes weekly.

www.ingramcontent.com/pod-product-compliance
Lightning Source LLC
Chambersburg PA
CBHW050752180726
48003CB00020B/2504